Stop those Pants!

Mordicai Gerstein

HARCOURT BRACE & COMPANY   San Diego   New York   London

Requests for permission to make copies of any part of
the work should be mailed to: Permissions Department,
Harcourt Brace & Company, 6277 Sea Harbor Drive,
Orlando, Florida 32887-6777.

Library of Congress Cataloging-in-Publication Data
Gerstein, Mordicai.
Stop those pants!/Mordicai Gerstein.
p. cm.
Summary: A young boy has trouble getting dressed one
morning when his clothes decide to play hard to get.
ISBN 0-15-201495-0
(1. Clothing and dress—Fiction.) I. Title.
PZ7.G325Sl 1998
(E)—dc20 96-44228

First edition
F E D C B A

Printed in Singapore

Dedicated with love to my grandson Hughgie,

who will never let his pants get away from him.

"Murray, are you up? It's time to get dressed!"

Murray woke up.

"Did you hear me?" his mother called from downstairs. "It's late."

"I'm up, Mom," yelled Murray. "I'm getting dressed."

Murray slid out of bed.

"Where are those pants?" he wondered. "I'm sure I left them on the chair."

He saw a pant leg sticking out from under his bed.

He grabbed for it, but it slid farther under.

"Get over here," Murray said to his pants.

"Why?" asked his pants.

"Because I have to get dressed."

"Why?" asked his pants.

"Cut that out and come here!" said Murray.

"Can't make me!" said his pants, hopping onto the bed.

"Besides, you don't even have your underwear on yet."

"Oops . . . you're right," said Murray.

The pants bounced on the bed.

Murray took off his pajamas and looked in his drawer.

"Any clean underwear in here?" he asked.

"NO!" yelled a chorus of little voices, and out jumped all his socks.

"I see you," Murray said to the underwear he saw hiding under a T-shirt.

"Where are we going today?" asked the underwear.

"School," said Murray.

"Not again!" wailed the underwear.

"Stop wriggling!" said Murray. "I can't get you on."

"Guess who?" asked the pants, as they jumped on Murray's head.

"Get off!" said Murray.

"Catch me!" giggled the pants.

"I will!" yelled Murray.

"We'll help!" cried the socks.

They chased the pants over the bed and around the room.

"Wear *me*, Murray," said his new gorilla T-shirt. "I'm good at catching pants."

"You couldn't catch a cold, FUR FACE!" jeered the pants from the light fixture.

"*I'm* going to catch a cold if I don't get dressed," said Murray, putting on the T-shirt.

"A GORILLA!" shrieked the socks, and hid under the bed.

"Look at Murray
the monkey!"
whooped the pants.
"His shirt's on
backward!"

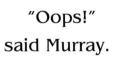

"Oops!"
said Murray.

He struggled
to turn the shirt
around.

"Careful!"
shrieked the shirt.
"You're twisting my
arm!"

"Sorry,"
said Murray.

"Wait'll you're put in the washer," sneered the pants.
"You'll see what twisted is . . ."

"You'll never get *me* in the washer again," the pants crowed.

"Come on, you guys!" Murray said to his clothes. "Help!"

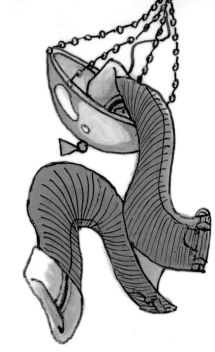

"I'll get him down," said Murray's cowboy belt. "Make me into a lasso, and we'll rope him!"

"Good plan," said Murray.

"Nyah! Nyah!"
jeered the pants.

Murray made a lasso, twirled it, and . . .

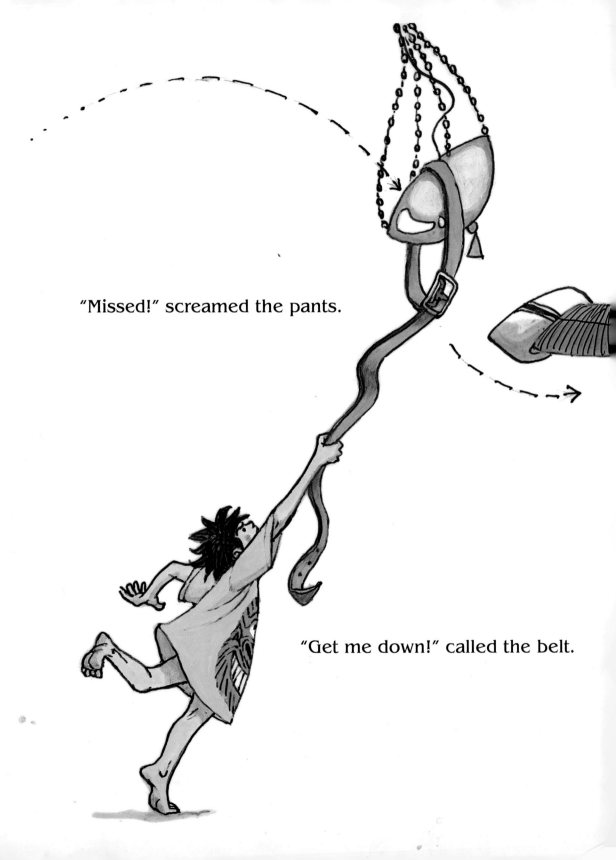

"This is FUN!" yelled the pants.

"I love FUN! I've been
BORED! I want to
JUMP, LEAP, RUN . . .
I'm sick of SITTING!"

"I feel the same
way," said Murray.

"Murray!" came his mother's voice. "Breakfast is on the table!"

"Look," Murray said to his pants, "I'll run all the way to school. I'll roll down the biggest hill in the park on the way home. I'll fill your pockets with wonderful things. Please come down."

"What wonderful things?" asked the pants.

"Pennies,
pistachios,
puzzles . . ."
"What else?"

". . . seashells,
a flashlight,
a race car . . ."

"What else?" asked the pants.
". . . nail clippers, a tiny Swiss
army knife, and . . ."
"YES?"

"I LOVE YO-YOS!" cried the pants. "LET'S GO!"

"YAAY!" cheered Murray's belt and shirt and socks and underwear.

The pants jumped
onto Murray's legs.

"Are you ready
for us?" asked his
socks.

"One purple and one orange, please," said Murray.
The socks leaped onto his feet.

"Sneakers!" called Murray.

"Is it time to go?" yawned the right one. "I overslept."

"Where's your partner?" asked Murray.

"How should I know?" said the sneaker, and hopped onto Murray's foot. "Regular knot or double?"

"Double," said Murray, looking around the room while his shoe tied a neat double knot.

"MURRAY!" his mother shouted. "This is IT! Come down and have your breakfast. Your left sneaker is under the table waiting for you!"

"We're coming!" called Murray and his underwear and pants and shirt and socks and belt and right sneaker.

And they all slid down the banister to breakfast.

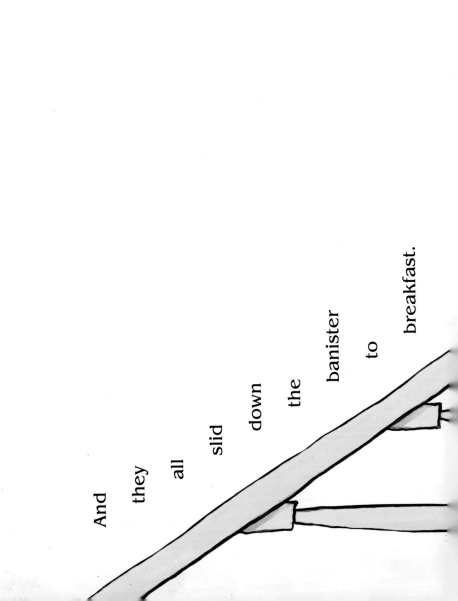

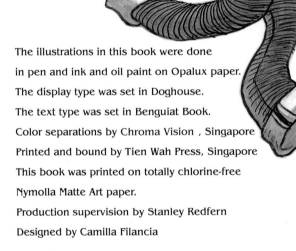

The illustrations in this book were done
in pen and ink and oil paint on Opalux paper.
The display type was set in Doghouse.
The text type was set in Benguiat Book.
Color separations by Chroma Vision , Singapore
Printed and bound by Tien Wah Press, Singapore
This book was printed on totally chlorine-free
Nymolla Matte Art paper.
Production supervision by Stanley Redfern
Designed by Camilla Filancia